D1145036

Feather Pillows

To Graham,
in memory of Dora
RI

For the staff and pupils
at Great Dalby Primary School,
Leicestershire
RBC

Robin Bell Corfield would like to thank the following people for their help in posing for characters in this book:
the pupils at Great Dalby Primary School, Mary and Helen Hulbert, Mark, Carole, Briony and Thomas Bendle,
Martin and Debbie Burke, Danielle Mayes, Pauline Hogg, and Sue Oliver and Ruth Corfield.

First published in Great Britain by HarperCollins Publishers Ltd in 1997. ISBN: 0 00 198139-0
10 9 8 7 6 5 4 3 2 1 Text copyright © Rose Impey 1997. Illustrations copyright © Robin Bell Corfield 1997
Printed in Singapore

Feather Pillows

Rose Impey

Illustrated by
Robin Bell Corfield

Collins
An Imprint of HarperCollinsPublishers

Sarah was bored with the adults talk-talk-talking.

They'd been sitting round the table ever since dinner finished,
Mum and Dad and Grandpa and Uncle Alan and Auntie Sissie –
talking and laughing and crying.

It was all right for Jake; he was being amused. They were passing him round like a parcel. But Sarah was a big girl; she was expected to amuse herself.

She had enjoyed it at first
when Mum suggested getting
out the photos. There were
lots of Mum and Auntie Sissie
when they were little;
sometimes she couldn't tell
which was which.

Sarah's favourite was the one of them paddling in a duck-pond, with their dresses tucked in their knickers.

And Sarah had enjoyed seeing the photos of Grandma Dora, especially the one of Grandma holding her when she was a tiny baby. Sarah was crying so hard, her face was screwed up like a little walnut, but Grandma was looking at her as if she was the most beautiful baby in the world.

Sarah had enjoyed the stories too, especially the one about how untidy Mum was when she was a girl. Once Grandma had got so cross with her that she'd opened the bedroom window and thrown all Mum's clothes onto the front lawn, just as Mum was walking home from school with her friends.

But now everyone was starting to get sad and talk about
Grandma's illness which made Sarah remember that Grandma
Dora had died and wasn't just away somewhere visiting, as she
sometimes liked to think she was.

Sarah tugged at Mum's sleeve for attention.

"Why don't you go and play in the garden, Sweetie," said Mum.

"No one to play with,"
Sarah grumbled.

"Take Jake," said Dad.

Uncle Alan stood Jake on the floor.

"All right," said Sarah. "Come on."

She led Jake down the six steps into Grandpa's garden.

On the last step Jake sat down with a bump and picked up an empty snail shell. He poked his finger inside as far as it would go. Sarah took the shell away from him.

"Stop that, Jake," she said, "it's dirty. You'll catch germs if you're not careful."

Sarah led Jake across the lawn, into the shade of an apple tree.

Jake started to pull at his shoes.

"No, leave them on," she told him. "Look at this instead."

Sarah showed Jake the photo Grandpa had given her of Grandma in a deckchair with an ice-cream. There was a donkey's head appearing over Grandma's shoulder as if it was about to eat the cornet. It was taken on holiday, before Jake was born.

"This is your Grandma, I mean *was* your Grandma," she told
him. Jake tried to take the photo but Sarah moved it away
in case he creased it. She gave him a silver sweet wrapper out
of her pocket instead; Jake put it straight into his mouth.

"Oh, no you don't," she said, sounding exactly like her mum.

Jake looked at her, puzzled for a moment. Sarah laughed
and pushed him onto his back and rolled him over and over

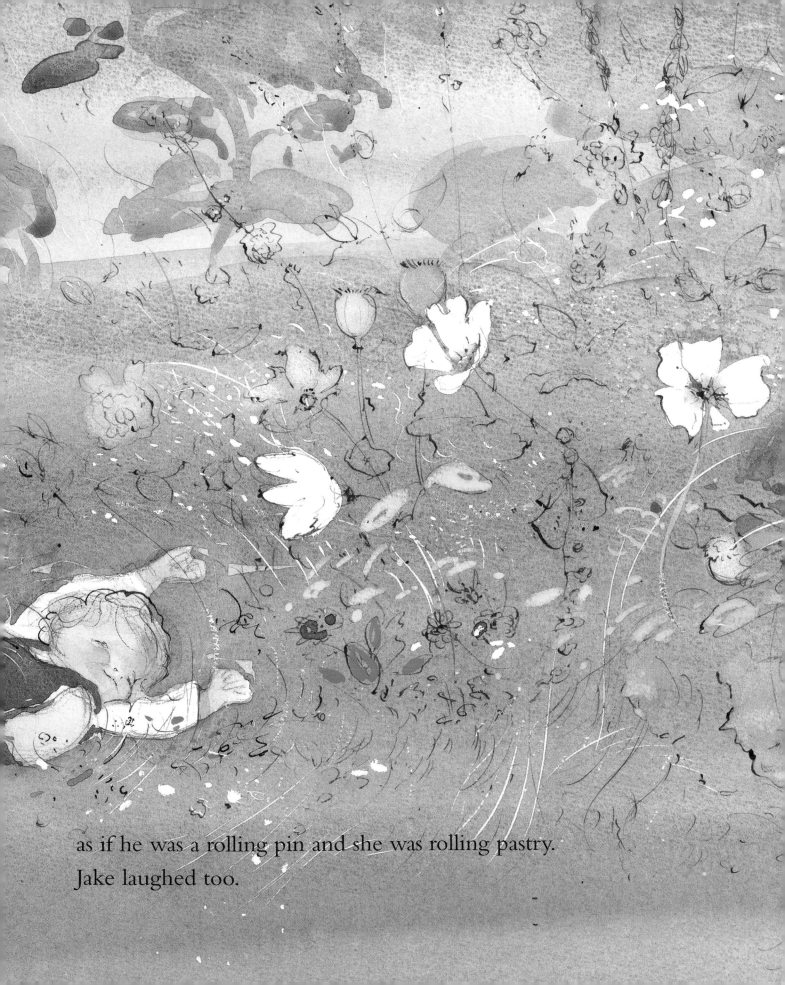

as if he was a rolling pin and she was rolling pastry.
Jake laughed too.

A blackbird landed close to them on the grass. Then Sarah remembered Grandma playing 'two little dicky birds sitting on a wall'. Grandma used to tear two little strips of newspaper and wrap them round her fingers, wetting the ends to make them stick. The way she made the birds appear and disappear was like a magic trick. Sarah tried to do the trick, with pieces of grass instead, but Jake got bored and crawled away from her over the lawn.

At the end of the garden
was a little brick outbuilding.
Jake banged on the door and
rattled the handle, but nothing
happened.

"No use knocking," said
Sarah, "nobody lives there."

But Jake went on rattling
hopefully. Sarah gave the door
a push and Jake tumbled in
and burst out crying.
She tried to comfort
him, but Jake pushed
her away.

Inside the little house was a lawn-mower and a wheelbarrow, deckchairs and a couple of old bikes that Mum and Auntie Sissie used to ride. Jake tried to climb into the wheelbarrow. Sarah tugged his nappy and he rolled in and curled up, with his thumb in his mouth.

"You mustn't go to sleep," said Sarah. She pulled out his thumb, but Jake stuck it back in.

It was cool in the little house and quiet. The sun's rays came slantwise through the windows. Thousands of specks of dust quivered in the light, as if they were alive.

On the window-sill, Sarah spotted
a tiny white feather. She picked
it up and tickled herself on the
end of her nose with it. She
remembered a day, before Jake
was born, when he was still in
Mum's tummy, a hot day, just
like this one.

Sarah and Mum and Grandma Dora came down to the little
house to make feather pillows out of Great Grandma's feather
bed. They were all wearing old clothes and scarves tied round
their hair, to keep the feathers out. Sarah wore an apron of
Grandma's with two pockets full of lavender.

When they cut open the feather bed, hundreds of tiny feathers
flew up in a cloud, getting up Sarah's nose and making it itch.
Mum and Grandma took handfuls and pushed them deep into
the pillowcases. Each time they called her,
Sarah came and sprinkled in handfuls
of lavender, to make the pillows
smell sweet.

When they were full, Mum and Grandma sat on stools and
sewed up the pillows, with tight little stitches to keep the feathers
in, while Sarah chased feathers out of the door, into the sunlight.

Sarah looked round at Jake, snoozing in the wheelbarrow. She stroked the inside of her arm with the feather. It tickled and made her laugh, even though there were two little tears running down her face. It felt funny, laughing and crying at the same time.

Suddenly, Sarah could feel eyes on her. In the doorway were Mum and Dad and Uncle Alan and Auntie Sissie, all watching her.

"I see Jake's asleep again," said Dad.

"What have you been doing?"
asked Mum.
    "Thinking."
    "Nice thoughts?" asked Dad.
Sarah nodded.
    "So what's making you cry?"
    "Feather pillows," said Sarah.
    "Ahhh," said Mum.

And she scooped Sarah
up, as big as she was, and
hugged her very tight.
And Sarah tickled Mum's
nose with the feather and
they both laughed and cried,
at the same time.